Published in hardcover by Alyson Wonderland,
an imprint of Alyson Publications, Inc., 40 Plympton St., Boston, Mass. 02118.
Distributed in England by GMP Publishers, P.O. Box 247, London N17 9QR, England.

First edition, first printing: July 1993

2 4 5 3 1

ISBN 1-55583-205-9

UNCLE WHAT-IS-IT IS COMING TO VISIT!!

by Michael Willhoite

Boston ♦ Alyson Wonderland
an imprint of Alyson Publications, Inc.

To Lisa and Alan

"Tiffany!"
No answer.
"Igor!"
No answer.
No *way!* My sister Tiffany and I
were hiding in our treehouse. Hiding
from Mom. It was lunchtime, and we
were as hungry as grizzly bears.
There was just one problem: brussels
sprouts. I'd seen Mom in the kitchen
chopping off their stems when Tiff
and I were going out to the back
yard. Yuck!!

"Tiffany! Igor! It's time for lunch!"

"What'll we do?" asked Tiffany. "She knows where we are."

"You don't *know* that — be quiet!" I hissed. "Maybe she'll go away."

"Well, I'm hungry." Tiffany is eight, a year younger than me. When you're eight years old, you're hungry all the time.

"Tiffany, Igor, why are you still in that treehouse? Lunch is ready — fried chicken."

We hit the ground and ran for the house.

There was the chicken, all right — a heaping platter of it. And a bowl of creamy potato salad. And iced tea.

Tiffany grabbed for a leg.

"Don't start yet," said Mom. "The brussels sprouts are still cooking ... And don't look so miserable. They're good for you."

We didn't believe her and she knew it. "Look, kids, I've got some great news for you." Mom pulled a letter from her apron pocket. "Your Uncle Brett is coming tomorrow. He's going to stay for a few days."

"Who's Uncle Brett?" Tiffany asked.

"He's my brother. He lives in Boston, but before that he lived in London. He hasn't seen you since you were just babies."

"London, England?" I asked.

"What does he look like?"

"Does he like baseball?" This was *very* important. I *love* baseball.

"One question at a time!" said Mom. "Yes, he lived in London, England, and yes, Igor, he likes baseball a lot. He played in high school. I may have a picture of him in his uniform somewhere in the attic..."

"Is he married?"

Mom got sort of a funny look on her face. "No, Tiffany, he's not married. Well ... as a matter of fact, he's gay."

"What's that?" we asked at the same time.

Mom's eyes popped wide open, as black smoke started billowing out of the kitchen. "Good lord! The brussels sprouts!" She dashed out to the stove.

After lunch, Tiff and I were walking to the playground behind the Baptist church, five blocks away.

"I can hardly wait to meet this Uncle Brett," I told Tiffany. "Maybe he'll play catch with me." Dad never seemed to have time.

"Igor." She stopped. "What is 'gay'? We never found out."

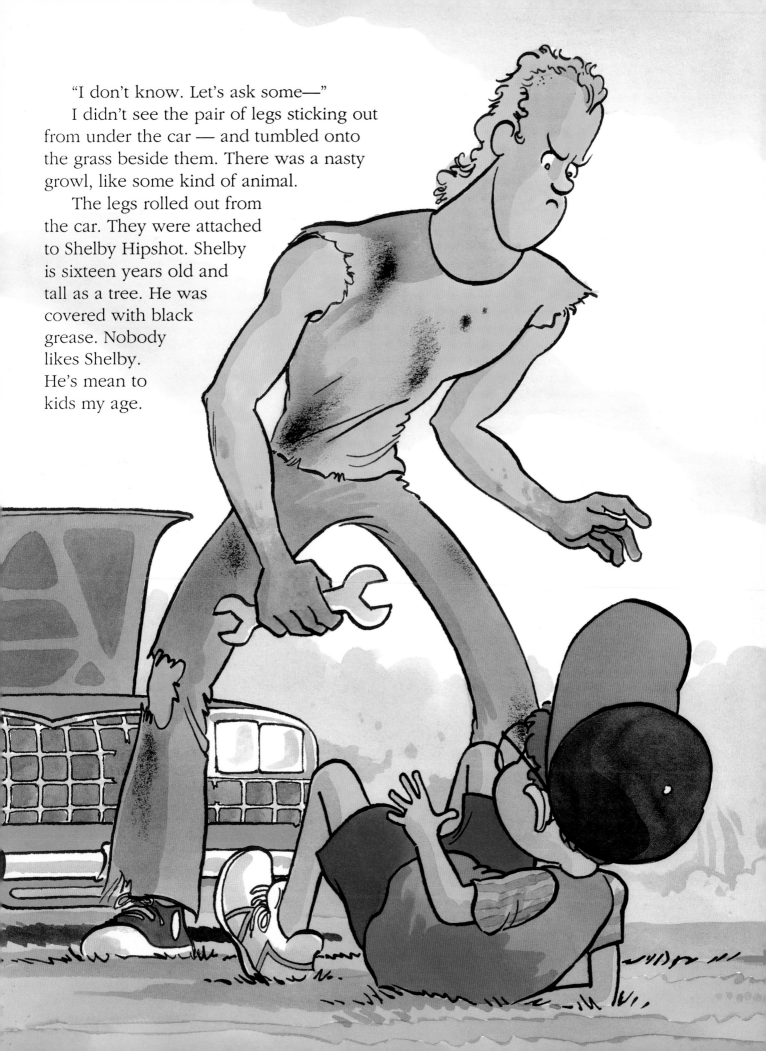

"I don't know. Let's ask some—"

I didn't see the pair of legs sticking out from under the car — and tumbled onto the grass beside them. There was a nasty growl, like some kind of animal.

The legs rolled out from the car. They were attached to Shelby Hipshot. Shelby is sixteen years old and tall as a tree. He was covered with black grease. Nobody likes Shelby. He's mean to kids my age.

Shelby grabbed me by the shirt. "Why don't you watch out, slimeball? I don't appreciate gittin' stomped on."

"I ... I'm sorry! I was talking to my sister. We—"

"What were you talking about that's so important?"

"Our Uncle Brett," piped up Tiffany. She looked pretty scared — and said the first thing that popped into her head: "He's gay."

Shelby dropped me like a used Kleenex and turned to Tiff. He smiled and gave a nasty little snicker. She looked even *more* scared.

"Hey, Waldo. Did you hear that? These kids got an uncle that's a fag!" There was a laugh from the other side of the car. Waldo was Shelby's brother. The more Waldo and Shelby laughed, the madder I got. Tiffany looked unhappy.

Shelby saw her and stopped. "Aaaww..." he whined, "Poor little baby's got a queer uncle ... We shouldn't laugh, Waldo." Waldo stopped laughing too.

Shelby got real friendly. "Hey, let me tell you about gay guys."

Hmmm ... Shelby may have been a geek, but he *might* be able to tell us something. We sat down on the curb.

"They really want to be women."

"What?" I couldn't quite believe this.

"Yeah, sometimes they even dress up in women's clothes. Look." A stack of newspapers were nearby, for use as paper towels. He pulled one from the pile. "GAY PRIDE PARADE," read a small headline. Underneath was a news photo of a large man dressed in a frilly dress. A turban piled high with fruit sat on his head.

"Coochy, coochy, coochy," squealed Shelby. With hands on his hips, he danced around the lawn. Was *that* what Uncle Brett was like?

Oh, no!
I grabbed Tiffany by the hand. "Let's get out of here!" We raced down the street. Behind us, Shelby and Waldo were laughing their heads off.

In front of Old Man Wosky's house we stopped. Tiffany was crying. "Oh, Igor," she wailed. "I don't want Uncle Brett to come!"

"Now wait, Tiff. You know what Shelby's like. Maybe he was just being a jerk — like usual. How do we know he's telling the truth?"

Footsteps were suddenly behind us. I turned around. It was Waldo.

"Hey, kids..." He stopped to catch his breath.
"Aaaaahh ... that Shelby's crazy," he finally
gasped. "They ain't nothin' like that." He took a
deep breath. "I seen a bunch of 'em once, when I
was in Chicago."

He sat Tiff and me down on Old Man
Wosky's front step. He didn't snort and giggle
and act like a doofus like Shelby. Maybe we were
really going to get the straight scoop.

"Yeah, they're not like that at all. The ones I seen were dressed up in black leather. Zippers and chains all over 'em. Dark glasses ... Chaps!"

"Like cowboys?" I asked. Hey, cowboys weren't so bad.

"Well, not exactly. You know what the Hell's Angels are like?"

"The Hell's Angels!!!"

"Yeah — like that. They call 'em leather queens." He got up off the sidewalk, popped a Life Saver into his mouth, and turned to go back to work on the car.

"You kids — any time you want to know somethin', you come to Waldo." He sauntered back down the street.

At dinner that night we didn't say much. All
Dad talked about was business. Every time Mom
mentioned Uncle Brett, I'd start to ask a question. But then I'd look at Tiff's unhappy face
and shut up. Dinner was pretty miserable.
At least there weren't any brussels sprouts.
That night we wondered, *What in the
world* was coming
to visit tomorrow?

Next morning Tiffany and I were up in
our room. Waiting. Waiting for — what? A
taxi pulled into the driveway.

We looked down, but the branches
from the elm tree were in the way. "Well,
Igor, we might as well go down. Or he'll
just come up."

We sat at the foot of the stairs. We could hear Mom outside, laughing and talking to Uncle Brett. The knob turned. And...

"Are *you* Uncle Brett?" I asked.

"Are you really gay?" asked Tiffany. "Where's your fruit hat?"

"No, no — where's your black leather suit — you know, with the chains and stuff."

"Uncle Brett—"

"Tiffany! Igor!" Mom groaned. "What's gotten into you? Who told you all this?" She turned to Uncle Brett. "I don't know where they got these ideas!"

But Uncle Brett just laughed.

We found out a lot about Uncle Brett during the next few days. He can play catch better than Dad. *And* more often. He can wiggle his ears, play the piano, and make fancy desserts. He explained that gay men are just guys who fall in love with each other instead of with women. He said that women who fall in love with other women are called lesbians. He told us that some gay men *do* dress up like women and some *do* wear black leather. But that's all right, too.

Uncle Brett is *neat*. And...

He hates brussels sprouts too!

DEMCO

ALYSON
WONDERLAND